THE UNIFORM LIGHT

Bernie Ray Day Dawn

AuthorHouse™
1663 Liberty Drive
Bloomington, IN 47403
www.authorhouse.com
Phone: 833-262-8899

Because of the dynamic nature of the Internet, any web addresses or links contained in this book may have changed
since publication and may no longer be valid. The views expressed in this work are solely those of the author and do
not necessarily reflect the views of the publisher, and the publisher hereby disclaims any responsibility for them.

Any people depicted in stock imagery provided by Getty Images are models,
and such images are being used for illustrative purposes only.
Certain stock imagery © Getty Images.

This book is printed on acid-free paper.

ISBN: 978-1-4918-6968-0 (sc)
ISBN: 978-1-4918-6967-3 (e)

Print information available on the last page.

Published by AuthorHouse 03/31/2021

authorHOUSE®

Chapter 1 - Foundation

It's birth was pure in nature, clear of sight for it was lost and found again. Bright, shiny, gleaming with the magnificence of the ages yet still only a reflection of itself the presence moved with definition, seeking its purpose (the purpose that it had) knowing it would be delayed. Yet there was no worry. Whether be found or be absorbed into its surrounding fabric the result would be the same; a purification factor. The world needed cleansing in such a way that no one felt the guilt. Such was the path to take, give, and present.

To go any faster would give way to incompetence, certainly unheard-of (although time and time again people would complain). Seizing the advantage and carrying on in such a way that a mere child could appreciate the intelligence, the formation glanced quickly from side to side while surging forward with all the hype possible to muster.

Suddenly it happened! It repeated itself! Anyone hit that quickly with a ~pie(3.14)~ in the eye could realize it; yet gone and away it went in the manner of etiquette sufficient enough to please a king although a royal shuffle was to be found somewhere. But where?! Where did the bloomin' thing go?!! Exclusively out of sight in such a blinding speed that unnoticed, unrestricted and under a previous passage it went.

Ah, there the answer be. The clues could be found in the woods, the metallic stronghold, and the Opal city. The Opal city consisted of this; mellow absorbing materials that saturated in the wholeness of life. We begin the trace of the journey here.

Geecy Gatorchomp was feared the world over to to its outrageous appetite for the essentially physical Cee. Cee's ability to maneuver deftly through all sorts of near fatal predicaments was his fame. The land of the Opal city contain situations of proportion that only logic could cure. Cee moved prodigiously through the chambers of his analytic commutational region in search of another implement of craniumical settlement (usually a limlake or a gloc). He settled for a bowl of oatmeal. Finishing With dext ous dexterity he leaped upon his couch potato and took off

Ah, the Iekland. There was no better place to go in the summer than the Iekland. People eating limlakes or drinking gloc just sitting around playing a Chicago Stradivarius. A Holly ride was usually a sure cure for boredom. Oh well, nothing so drastic as to consult the Seer of the Past. Maybe the Referrer or another fine gent would perchance the road and make the day interesting.

Satisfaction was found in the form of the Referrer's mate. Glimpz moved uneasily across the road. She seemed distressed that her newly found longest hair would only jostle in the wind when surrounding threadlike outgrowths did. Cee remedied this by caressing each one and returning them to their original first-seen position.

Suddenly everyone was gone! A beagle appeared! Funny lookin' thing! It made its way toward the bowling alley and sat for a gloc with a bent cavalier while waiting to test its skill on the lanes of endeavor. Such was found a truly enjoyable day. Arrows and dots and balls and extravagant usage of the finer things of life. People looked from miles around.. The Seer of the Past appeared. Limlake wrappers disappeared.

Glimpz and the Referrer wished they could calculate their position. Fine if they proceeded in an orderly fashion toward cloth and material gain. Cee appeared. Guiding the unison in an intricate collaboration of profound maneuver they became an entourage of bricklifying embodiment of glamorous spectacle. There they were.

They became aware of the presence of shimmering crystal illuminated through the power of a mysterious force. Patterns formed on the walls and carried and announced message intriguing to the beholder. The Referrer looked at Cee quizzically and wondered if there might be a chance at interpretation. Glimpz like the colors. Discussing the possibilities of solution 'twixt themselves they rendered a decision to isolate the common factors of each segment.

One segment contained a mathematical sequence of musical harmony. Using a scale of 1 to 150 of the range of intensity audible by the human ear converted from the varying intensity of shock generated it sounded just like a 1960's rock 'n roll tune, or maybe something from Woodstock; at third guess maybe a primate thumping sound.

Another segment seemed to condition air movement. Crystal upon crystal floated buoyantly while filtering gaseous movement. Shimmering fluctuations seem to produce a comfortably

A third segment displayed fountainous liquid formations. Level upon level of intricate patterns formulated tributarious entourages pleasing to the beholder. Such magnificence and excellence! Such breathtaking beauty! The Referrer seemed shaken. He staggered first right, then left, then forward catching hold of a fourth segment with his right hand unknowingly releasing a savage force!! Gatorchomp attacked with a vicious flurry of tooth and fang development unrivaled for centuries past in the direction of a panic stricken, wide-eyed with terror, unable to hold onto the ceiling with bone white wrenching fingernails Glimpz!!!

Cee miraculously put use of an oodle of might (an oodle is a unit of strength quantified by powers of ten, named after the oodle, a legendary creature much like the unicorn) to force open the door to the woods. He quickly ushered Glimpz out of Gatorchomp's path, resumed her relation with the Referrer and shut the door on a wild eyed, half crazed, somewhat shattered, partially stunned, out of tune, junk piled, ready for the compactor Creecy Gatorchomp.

The Woods opened to enfold the Referrer and Glimpz. They caressed each other in marital bliss. Penetration of involvement occurred. Each in each, then in then; time passage.

Chapter 2 - Band

Once upon a time in the Lapland of the Woods, Cee met Bluegrass for a jam session of unequaled quality. On bass was Thickthumb because for many a year he played rhythemous scales along with chords. On drums was Bong just because he liked the sound of him. On lead guitar was Bluegrass because he could play behind his back with his eyelashes. Cee played rhythm guitar.

The lawn began to team with excitement as people got acquainted with places to occupy. The vendors were spilling their products, making catches were purchasers of the Loyal Togetherness. Gloc and limlakes you ask? Of course! is the triumphant answer.

The special of the day was Jippsyum (pay for the newness). A grade A treat that one could lay into at the Rock Garden.

The show began to be introduced by a reasonable facsimile of the largest man on the planet (was it really him?) projecting a bellow without a microphone, making sure everyone could hear him; "Announcing the highly emotional, extra-sensational, ready to take the stage: A Band!"

Hit the high strings wake up the light, the Earth is in for a party today, the day is here, the fun is ours, nobody stops us on the earth, moon, or Mars. "What day is it?", they started to scream. Never mind you, it's just a dream of ice cream and raisins and soda cups. Just look around us, it's all mixed up. Today without effort our band's so complete that inside our heads keep on spinning. We've got bells on our feet. Our day is good, our brunch is fine, we'd even call you if we had a dime plus whatever it takes to keep a telephone going. In this pleasant hour will just take to have lunch because it's our custom to eat our food with our heads on straight. We could still read the news on the bright written headlines that tell us the way of the future and prospect and total array that's keeping us with this and here on display with promise and feeling while we're in the mood that we just keep on playing through lunch midday snack food dinner each morsel we eat that we keep on playing. Our stage is today that our notes bring harmonies. Our structure is fast in accapello or tremolo our notes just go in the hopes the Big Fellow; (the largest man on the planet that introduced him) will let us play through all this day, afternoon through twilight where this place that we jam still stays open all night to next day we play everything's still together our equipment make is Woods, Metallic Stronghold, and Opal City.

The stage slowly fogged as a fine mist began to flow over the lower extremities of the performers. The lights lowered and an eerie silence spread over the spectators and bandmembers alike. Cee stepped up to center stage, raised his arms and announced "and now, our sequel to Godspell".

Lightning flashed across the stage as the guitars toned a sustained sound while the drums kept a steady, mounting beat. Cee recounted history in song as he sung about previous terrestrial crashes, the technology derived in the escalation of human-kind all the way to the God-like sighting of the Hubbel astronauts and the standards of man reaching a well-learned status from lessons previously taught. Thick and Blue blended background harmonies as Cee defined the subtle differences between the writings of the Bible and the more recent interpretations of the moral codes.

"The early tribes blended into believers of all types of nations, races and colors. They wrote of their history and much of it still pertains truths to our more recent times. In the beginning good orderly direction formed heaven and earth, caused light to appear, seeded, produced yield, brought forth creatures to multiply: to what extent the landmass-creature ratio is vague, a standard could be helpful".

The video monitor shifted to scenes of early population as Cee continued. "The early people of Earth chose their roles and proceeded to their lands, avoiding eating shellfish and cloven animals along the way; today we eat such cooked or prepared properly; resting on Saturday: most likely picking one full day each week where someone could sleep the day away would be appropriate. Some needed help from a higher power". Cee smiled and interjected, "Didn't they see the starcraft?" "They lived by 10 laws, now that's taking it to a t: what way do they turn at the end of the T? Some managed agreements with these higher power". The music turned to the form of a high energy city train sound, historic scenes flashed on the monitors. "There were priests and sons of priests living certain ways"; "How vane is close to the vein and what should go up in smoke?" "The people divided into tribes, marrying among their own; try that today", he snickered. " They renewed their law, founded settlements, renamed a leader, heeded mighty deeds. Widows were remarried. A higher power dwelt in a mountain, nations were judged against, a kingdom chosen, a fish swallows a man and casts him to land. A prophet foretells a Messiah in the style of his mentor. A king chased an annointed, an ark retrieved a king receives wisdom, a great temple is built and maintained, genealogy is documented. Tribes revolt, people fast for a right way, wall their city, display patience". "Getting all this?" Cee mused. "Their laments are abated, an adopted becomes queen, sufferings endured in faith. Praises are written, counsel is found in parables, vanity examined. Love proclaimed, wisdom sought, virtues taught, the prophet asks for conversion; people are warned, sorrow expressed alphabetically, prayer requested in atone for sins." "There's more!" "Prophecies were spoken, a wise man delivered from a lion's den, the lesser prophet preaches repent and redemption, a city is destroyed, land invaded, idolatry punished, a new temple built, blessings promised, new sacrifices accepted, people fight and horsemen running in the air".

"That brings us to the four wise guys". The music raised to a sustained crescendo while the effects portrayed an eternal uniform light. "They each told the news of a Mentor, Hero, Savior in their own way; the first focusing his countrymen, the second and third to converts, the last at the request of elders". "Who inspired these guys?", Cee mused. The lighting returned to a more natural setting, the music to a march. "Let's bring it on home!", Cee rumbled. "The establishment, reward and punishment, moral disorders corrected, offenders pardoned and preachings not of man". "Ah, now we're getting somewhere.", Cee continued. "A mystical body, a minister for liberation, the rules for life, constant faith, idleness discouraged". "Musn't dally", Cee quipped. " false teaching opposed, an example set, leadership instructions given, a plea for a fugitive: a new dispensation, faithful living encouraged, more faithfulness exhorted, warnings against falsehoods". "The expression of light, justice and love; brotherly love. Some are praised and some are censored, holy perseverance, the end of the world described". A triumphant chord rang out as Cee explained that the performance was based on a book of moral codes that was a way to begin a civilization. He continued that some of the circumstances may vary over time although at least there was a general rule book. "And there you have it! How else would you impart knowledge to a beginning civilization?" Cee bowed and was lifted offstage by the uniform light. The band continued to conclude the performance.

They swam and swam all over the stoppage of water through flowing yet in some wonderful place of places. Anywho, Screechborf ran around to clean up the place (who else would do it?). Then they went on to newer and better things because Screechborf on the clean team was only part of the solution of cleaning the pollution that happens at these "Announcing the highly

Meanwhile, back on the parent ship Cee discussed the concert with some old friends; especially Artie and his son. They pondered potential amendments such as a day of rest with pay and that a spouse could be able to please themself elsewhere as long as their mate was satisfied and that no undo jealousy was imposed. Financial gain from such gestures might deem consideration. Cee then played a private concert on his acoustic for them consisting of four songs.

WOODS PARTY - (D)Well we're out in the sun and we're having fun   It is (Em)gonna be a great day   (D)We've got our heads in the clouds and were singin' out loud   'Cause we (Em)know that we're here to stay   (A)for the day or a year   Doesn't matter if from far or near   (open)Time is here for you to hear   That this song is going in high gear   (D)There's a frisbee game and the people are sane   And they (Em)like to act crazy   (D)And they're out to explore or to talk some lore   Or (Em)just to catch some rays   (A)That's the way of the day   And everything seems to be okay   (open)And at night it's outta sight   We'll be takin' things to a new height   (D)Well we'll get on the phone after the dial tone   And (Em)talk to some ol' friends   (D)A conversation without complications   (Em)You know can sometimes send   (A)One away to partay   With a little or a lot to say   (open)Or some rest might be the best   To send one dreaming of another day   (C)Of the rich and the poor   (Am)Of the faithful and the shure   (G)If you find yourself thinking only of yourself beware

STOP SIGN - (A)Smokin' at the (G)stop (A)sign   And no one's a-(G)round   (A)A carnival's in the (G)back-(A)ground   It's a brand new (G)sound   (G)-(A),(G)-(A)

(A)Lookin' at the (G)wo-(A)men   They're lookin' mighty (G)tight   (A)Gonna find a (G)clear (A)line   And refreshingly get out of (G)sight   (A)They were lookin' at me I was (G)lookin' at them I was lookin' at them they were (A)lookin' at me   (A)We're (G)gone   It started (A)smokin' at the (G)stop (A)sign   (G)-(A),(G)-(A)   (A)Now I'm her's and she's (G)mine   (A)And you know we've got the (G)green (A)light   (G)-(A),(G)-(A)   (A)And I'm glad I seen the (G)sign   (A)She was lookin' at me (G)I was lookin' at her   I was lookin' at her (A)she was lookin' at me   (A)We're (G)gone   (G) We're (A)gone

MAD CAP JACK - (G)Now this here's the story 'bout a (A)drinkin' (G)man   Seen early in the mornin' with a (A)glass in his (G)hand   A few hours later he could (A)barely (G)stand   (C)I wonder now if you could guess his name   (chorus)(C)Well he is (G)Mad (A)Cap (G)Jack   And you know he's got his (A)un-(E)capped (A)Jack   (G)Mad (A)Cap (G)Jack   (A-F-G)And one thing he can tell you is a bottle'l do(end chorus)   (G)Now if you meet him sober he's the (A)nicest (G)guy   But you just gotta watch him when he (A)starts to (G)fly   You can tell his condition just by (A)sayin' (G) hi   (C)And then you'll know if he'll be wild or tame   (chorus)   (G)Now on a certain day Jack was (A)feelin' (G)mean   Drinkin' ol' number 7 'til the (A)glasses were (G)clean   He got a hit harder than as (A)if by Jim's (G)beam   (C)And he knew that Mr. Daniels was the one to blame   (chorus) (G)Now after that punch Jack was (A)seein' (G)double   And he knew he didn't want to cause (A) any (G)trouble   So he picked himself up from (A)out of the (G)rubble   And he (C)hoped that he would never feel the same   (chorus)

COSMIC FABRIC - (D)Out in the (G)distance of (A)far away (D)space   There lives a (G)being (A) born of love and (D)grace   He is sad this (G)day   His (A)mate passed (D)away   And the chill of the (G)night (A)brings a dismal (D)day   (chorus)(G)And so he formed a blanket from the (A) cosmic fabric of the (G)universe   In the hopes to dispell the cold and (A)lonely feeling of his (G) freezing curse   (D)The blanket (G) formed pure (A)ener-(D)gy   An inner (G)peace (A)blessed the enti-(D)ty   The colors (G)glowed both (A)white and (D)blue   And that peace now (G)spreads to (A)me and (D)you

Everyone enjoyed the ancestral mode songs and bid Cee farewell as Cee returned to his companion party.

The Seer of the Past appeared and tried to re-instigate the mess that just happened though the new arrangement was made of such an integral complexity that it lasted any such spell brought against it. He got tired and went home.

"The woods are just too exciting for me" it was heard Glimpz say and they found themselves transported [the Woods do that you know] to Gateland; not to be confused with the bowling alley that is in the Iekland of the Opal City; although most trails lead to these 3 places; just take the transporter (it's faster) [you'll see (Cee?)].

Chapter 3 - Metal

The wrought iron engravings of the archways and portals of Gateland of The Metallic Stronghold were ornamentally functional with provision for storage of tool and utensil to do nearly any sort of art and craft. There they were with columnous height and continuous weight. Structure dense and solid as the strongest of metal were they. Each column sturdily envisioned force of great proportion that strengthened a two-fold placement of stature.

Gateland appeared dismal, in need of some restoration though it was the place to be. (Gatorchomp was closing in earlier and would have a rougher plot engaging the group in new surroundings.) What new twist would be wrought about in these territories? Cee led them through the pathways of folded and discarded iron of what once seemed to be the housings of an elite militia formed during the civil uprisings in local power struggles to increase the faith with what seemed to be a regime determined to gather a fortitude that might end in the progress of a successfully diligent attitude of a maker be aware society that could long endure. Some sort of camp would be needed. The tents went up and were finished just as the hail rained down cold and heavy. It was borscht day and the fires had to be moved to safety to avoid being extinguished; no easy task but well worth the effort for a true borscht eater. Strange place for such a meal though what with the toppled tables of the nearby diner called the beanery next to the factory that produced entranceways for the domiciles of the nearby towns and villages and tribal areas set aside for the recent encampments of what looked like the aftermath of a low scale citizen rebel against totalitarian regime nuclear rebellion. Usually nobody was much of a winner in the civil wars and most of any people remaining walked around like scavengers from an unemployment line with the exception of those factions retaining enough knowledge and materials to hold together a sort of think tank of custom to act as supply we're possible.

Appearing through the wreckage entered a Hogish dog. Well-dressed in a mutated sort of way, part human and part canine with a nose for borscht that could only be rivaled by its (his) stomach. He untoppled a table and produced a large quantity of his culinary preference thereupon whereasto enjoy a somewhat disturbed meal in quaint surroundings.

"Whatta 'ya doin' dog?"; Cee asked with quizzical concern. Unstartled due to its keen sense of sight the Hogish dog replied "feasting and yes you and your friends may join, though you'll probably owe me for this." "Shuck dog, 'tarin't a thing" replied Cee realizing that they should be good for something in these parts. Referrer and Glimpz relaxed slightly, Glimpz climbed down from atop Referrer's head, face and shoulders where he had supported her latest alarm, feeling kind of stressed yet intrigued at the effect he felt from Glimpz crossing her toes behind his back. They shuffled over to where Cee and dog were conversing.

"Come up for air, have you", said dog. "It's just as well, this Cee character hasn't said a sensible thing since he wandered over here. Maybe you two might prove a bit more entertaining". Cee shrugged and went off for some of this borscht himself. Course contain of nutritional compliment that even a lettuce eater would find appropriate for a fully balanced meal. Good food in such a case. Want for more? Yes, indeed!

The Hogish Dog began a conversation with Glimpz and The Referrer, inquiring first of their origins.

Chapter 4 - Beings

"We're both from lekland and lived on the same street, a short distance from the bowling alley" Glimpz offered. "We'd see each other when we played outside and got to know each other well through preliminary school. We later went to higher obligatory school and elective learning together. We've known each other all our lives!" "Yes", Referrer continued. " We went to proms together, were on bowling teams together, participated in afterschool activities together; we were quite the couple. Our training in related fields kept us together for life ambitions, mine as a soldier of fare and hers as a field operative. We were married three years after we began our occupations, we met Cee through our assignments."

"How interesting", said Dog. "What did you do for fun during these higher obligatory days?"

"Well", continued Referrer, "I'd pick up Glimpz after school in a box-wheel I used to own and we'd ride to the lakefront and park for a while, listening to tunes on a pieced together Z-loud Uhoidit sound system. We didn't have many credits and our parents weren't rich but they helped us when they could. Sometimes we'd pick up people we knew and make a night of it; talking, laughing, singing songs. Sometimes we'd bring some glock, limlakes, and jippsyum to share among us but we'd be careful not to over excess and get in trouble. An OE (over-excess) could cost thousands of credits and mess up a convenient lifestyle. We also went to movies, dance clubs, concerts and sporting events." "Referrer would also take me out to special dinners sometimes," Glimpz threw in. "I really liked the krimp and topster platters." "I see", acknowledged Dog and began to tell them about his life in Gateland.

"Gateland was once a proud place for us mutants, in fact for all who dwelt here. Most everything was based on the ore from the mines that was turned into structures occupying nearly the whole of the land and then some: structures below and above the surface. We'd trade our product dateland, being part of the Metallic Stronghold, formed more closely from another dimension than from a distance of area, as did Woods and Opal City. This all happened when the Terra planet underwent drastic geological and radiational changes. It is believed that flares from the central star bounced off a nearby planet reflecting Eramarsous radiation upon the terra type planet causing it to give birth to the three regions we presently occupy. Legend has it that this is where the origins of Mother Earth and men are from Mars are from. This is also when many mutant species were formed a few generations ago. Triangular markers were set to designate the areas the beam occurred at; I couldn't tell you if they exist today. It is known that other worlds were formed at the destruction of the original Terra formation, although it is said that the original planet still exists in some manner although the commuting apparatai don't seem to reach it." "I could remember many natural disasters throughout my childhood", Dog added. "Torrential rain storms would occur causing the structures to rust. The gates would shutter and periodically need to be realigned. There's plenty of maintenance in a city made of metal". "My father was mostly doggish and worked as a welder with the iron crews. My mother was earth-relative and made meals for the laborers at mid-day. They used to tell me stories of the old days. Factions would clash over land and building rights, regimes would rise and fall, taking over the structures of their predecessors and improving the architecture. Today the land is divided into metricities, each with a ruling faction and bands of rogueish citizens."

"Yo, Dog!" hailed Horker Magee as the Hogish Dog lept for the fences. "Calm down, calm down. It's just me and Turnip Oshanahee… mutant man-mutt and original party animal. We're just in from the concert and figured we'd camp out for a while." Horker Magee is acclaimed as the World's Greatest Partier, at least the people thought although there wasn't really a scale for accurate measurement. The Hogish Dog climbed down and smiled." So, you've decided to bless our humble stomping grounds with your most prestigious presence, have you? What's next on the agenda?", Dog queried." Enjoy the concert, did you?" Horker could not contain his enthusiasm. He rambled on about the amazing light show, the purity of the sound and the honorable presentation content. He then pointed off to the side and exclaimed "in large part to the actions of that formidable character peeking around off to the corner with an impish, satisfied look on his face in part from the recent delicious meal and moreover from the ambitious complement just paid to him." Cee acknowledged the praise and walked over to greet his old friends. "Horker, Turnip you know Dog, these are Referrer and Glimpz, you all get along spectacularly now, you hear?" Everyone chatted with one another a bit and were all

Chapter 5 - Peculiar Companions

Following the conversation a strange silence occurred. The Hogish Dog sensed danger. He sniffed at the air and frowned with recognition at an all too familiar smell, Landmazons, the female section of The Anvil Conglomerate, here to check on the recent commotion. "Now you did it" Dog toned. "Couldn't leave a peaceful meal as a peaceful meal. Now there's some 'splainin' to do". The members appeared from many different directions (all except the one Cee slid into). First Commoners, then Gruffs; Bravos and a few Arches. Finally in walked Kitty Wampass, the Chieftains wife, curviest girl of the tribe, her leathers barely containing her vivaciousness. "What have we here?"; she mused as she looked over the companions one by one. She shifted her stance in front of Turnip who sheepishly wet his loin cloth. She pointed to a makeshift latrine and commanded hurry back. "Happens more than I'd like to admit", she giggled. "And yet, there's still the matter of invasion of this locality. It's part of our station to keep an eye on things around here while the menfolk labor elsewhere. Have anything to say for yourselves?" Dog spoke up, being the most familiar with the situation. "I've seen you wandering here before", commented Kitty, "Out with it".

"Well, your heirarchy, only a few stragglers making their meager way across The Gateland, foraging here and there, planting where posible and improving the architecture where allowable".

"Vagabonds, ay? Well I guess you could earn some merit by laboring for The Anvil Conglomerate. Bravo Sunshine, issue these honorary Commoners work passes and assign details. We'll leave a few of us here while the rest forage and prepare for our menfolk. It everything goes well you'll be free to roam when we get back. We'll even issue travel passes".

"Thank you, m' lady. You won't be disappointed", chirped Dog.

Dog liked work. He could work like a dog when he wanted to and if there was a travel pass to be had, even though he didn't know what one was, he wanted one anyway and would work all the harder. He raised trellises, welded gates, formed seating areas and even helped raise the roof for the pavilion. Dog liked roof. His companions continued on a bit more melancholic but not altogether without zeal. After all, they wanted a travel pass too, whatever that was.

At nightfall the group huddled together off to the side to get some rest. Cee appeared to them and they told him of how they were working for a while to be issued travel passes. "Don't you want a travel pass too, Cee?", Glimpz inquired. "I don't need no travel pass" replied Cee. "I got my membership card to the etherial-material regions. Allows me to travel everywhere." "Oh, I see", mused Glimpz. "I'd like to see it sometime".

"Well, enough formalities for the time and being. There's an urgent matter that needs attention and I think The Anvils will actually be siding with us on this one. Word is that G. C. Gatorchomp is putting together a raid of a betrothal ceremony of which The Anvil Conglomerate is preparing a defense against".

Gatorchomp, game warden turned alligator mutant during the cataclysm still disliked too much freedom. Sometimes known as the freest of the free, Cee probably wouldn't resist a wonderful betrothal ceremony and that's what Geecy was planning on.

"We'll need to plan a defense ourselves to get through this one. I'll see if I could get in touch with the bandmembers and see if any of the following is versed in mercenarism. I have a few gems from some previous rewards that just might buy us the reinforcements we need. You keep on the good side with the Anvils and I'll be in touch soon". With that Cee was there one minute and gone the next. "How does he do that?", Referrer asked. They all shook their heads.

CHAPTER 6 - CAMP DUTY

Everyone woke to a new day of building and repair. The area of encampment was beginning to look like a veritable theater. "Okay, everyone up for work", rousted Fleet, Kitty's left arm Arch. "Work!", exclaimed Turnip in alarm who ran around in circles and latched on to Horker's right leg in fear. Horker slapped his forehead in distain and scuffled onward to meet the ensemble. "You two have been quite inconspicuous this past session. We'll try to find yous' something interesting today", commented Fleet. Horker MaGee shuffled off to the tool area in disgust. Turnip howled in grief and followed in line. Neither were much for manual labor and were trying hard to help out with their companions. Referrer, Glimpz and Dog reported for duty.

Cee, in his shimmering transparent form watched as Kitty met with her husband Bukalis. They had much to discuss. The men folk were in a good mood from the previous night's cuisine. The women's foraging went well and the menfolk had feral gore and iron plains hopper roasting on the pit and simmering in the kettle. The women's presentation resembled an inland luau and there was even music and dancing afterward. This led to other night time activity and everyone awoke relaxed and refreshed.

"So what's this I hear about trouble at the joining ceremony?", asked Kitty whose sources were not far less reliable than her husband's. "Terrible news, Kitty: Full spread invasion planned. We'll have some time to prepare and we should make good use of it. You remember G.C. and his bunch. He's also recruiting from the scattered ramblers of ill repute. We'll need allies ourselves and began a list of contacts. See who you could rustle up besides". "Yes dear", Kitty wiggled, producing a wry smile from her husband. "Well get going", said Bukalis Wampass, smacking her behind to urge her on. "Already have some ideas", commented Kitty as she strolled from the settlement.

The ladders went up around the pavilion. It was time to paint; keep the iron from rusting. First the primer and then the siliquer, both flexible and hard surfaced at the same time. Marvelous invention. Horker and Turnip were handed the first buckets and brushes and pointed to the wrought iron fence. "I've always wanted a green dog", commented Horker with a wry smile. "Thanks, Huckleberry", quipped Turnip. "Besides, you've seen me green before".

They climbed ladders, walked scaffolds, trimmed edges and although rarer and not totally absent poured concrete for steps and walkways. The band of workers broke for lunch, tried out the new hearth and continued on afterward. An Archamaeic lever principle was used to bring water to different parts of the structure and a series of aqueducts were used for plumbing. All in all a rather functional piece of architecture.

Screechborf appeared to help with the cleanup. How did he know where and when to help out? The Hogish Dog and Turnip Oshanahee conversed with Screechborf before he headed to his next assignment. They're all related you know.

During night time Kitty returned and began a grand opening ceremony for the outpost. They used the leftover paint and decorated their clothing, that what they left on, and chanted and danced resembling a scene from carnal knowledge. Afterwards she handed out the travel passes and asked them for their help in the upcoming conflict. They all agreed remembering the charge from Cee to obtain the help of the Anvils and any others they could procure.

Cee had his own reunions to tend to. He had the bandmember's liaisons meet him at an empty pavilion near one of the local towns. From here they could disperse and engage in skirmishes against the nearby hired bands of the opposing force. After a rousing pep talk Cee sent the troops on their way. Across the way Geecy Gatorchomp was doing the same.

Chapter 7 - Skirmishes

Quickfang ducked as Growlmonster swiped at his face. Groups of Metal-Blokes and Angle-Rangers booed and cheered depending on what side they were (confusing in battle), neither of which all too eager to join the fray until the outcome was decided. From his high ridge overlooking the territories each wanted to hold an advantage in observation. A quick slice to the neck with his bony oracles and a decisive end to the struggle was predicted! Not a fatal injury but one that would not allow the combatant to continue. Quickfang dialed up the exceptional ability of his travel pass and placed it on Growlmonster, instantly transporting him to the Radiation Depletion Camp in the Opal City. The travel pass returned and clanked at the victor's feet, ready for its next enlistment. A few Metal-Blokes and even a few Angle-Rangers struggled in disgust and then dispersed without the guidance of their leader. Quickfang felt relieved. The enhanced abilities from where the cosmic radiation of the Eramarsous Blast had concentrated on their ancestors was inherent in some of the opponents. Growlmonster hadn't been given too much chance to use his form shaking audible reverberation, although his large frame and intensified musculature were enough to deal with. The Depletion Camp would remove much of the radiation causing these developments and allow them a more realistic view of the world around them.

Strongfoot skirted the Rusty Marsh. He too had enhanced abilities from where the cosmic radiation of the Eramarsous Blast had concentrated on his ancestors. He used his abilities to further the causes of the greater good. Thump Ped used his for personal gain. Each traveled in groups of about 15 or 20 with their Metal-Blokes and Angle-Rangers, which was about the norm during these strenuous times. Strongfoot kicked a soccer ball over the marsh into some brush on the other side (he carried one in his pack for certain circumstances). It bounced off a Bloke, catching him on the side of the face who cried out in startled surprise. "Well, at least we know were they are now", commented Strongfoot. "Now what to do with them. I think we'll have to split up our forces, I don't like to but I think we'll have to. Half of you around that side, the other half with me. That side squad launch anything you could once you get there; Those with me keep as quiet as you could". The launch team rustled and tromped their way around.

Rocks and leaves and branches showered on the Thump faction who retaliated with a volley of makeshift arrows and spears. Few found any mark although the air above was turned to an untidy scattering of debris and weaponry. "Enough of this foolishness", boomed Thump Ped as he arranged his soldiers in a formation allowing him to use his signature move. He raised his foot, aimed in the direction of the approaching attackers and sent a shockwave through the ground, a ripple effect that toppled the aggressive activists. Seeing his chance Strongfoo charged in from the opposite direction and drop kicked the sturdy limb of the combatan sending him flying into a nearby Winepress tree rendering him unconscious. Activating the travel pass he flung it onto his opponent transporting him to the Radiation Depletion Camp The pass reappeared after depositing its load and Strongfoot reached over, collected it and once again attatched it to his shirt. As usual the ramble, without their leader, scattered to the surrounding areas. The winning faction executed a modest celebration of victory and returned to their duties.

Preparations were underway for months, some for years, for the betrothal ceremony of Baer and Romica in Ore Valley. Baer, a local mining magnate, was built like a rock and Romica, an ron forming heiress, had exquisite form. They would make a good-looking couple.

At the bansheen factory a large order of sweet bubbly was being produced for the reception party. Lowlimp snuck around through the glass bottles thinking of ways to sabotage the effort Bendedknee and his band of optimists was on guard aware of the disorder afoot. Soundlessly Lowlimp's crew made their way to the packing department. They would pierce the corks and grease the bottlenecks making the potable unusable for the reception. Bendedknee was astounded. "The fiends!", He whispered while sliding in circles with his arms waving wildly in the air. "We must do something immediately". Spying a pressurized bansheen vat with a valve pointing in the direction of his quarry Bendedknee jumped to the container, rappelled down the side and opened the valve releasing its contents upon his nemesis, pinning him to the corner with the force of the liquid. Then, using the rope he brought to steady himself, swung over in the deluge and tagged Lowlimp with a trusty travel pass. The crew shut the vat valve and as the overflowing subsided the travel pass reappeared and was reattached to its bearer. The angry mob disbanded in disgruntled fashion at the loss of their leader. Fortunately they weren't gruntled for too long.

In case you're wondering what has become of our group of chosen, after the opening ceremony at the outpost Kitty asked them to cover the dress shop. "We heard some Rosie Girls and Wande Groupies under the command of Miss Slink are headed there", explained Kitty. "Are you up for the mission?" "I've never been on a mission before", said Glimpz. "I hope it's not too dangerous". "We've got you", said Dog and was joined in supportive agreement by the rest of the company.

Miss Slink perused the dress shop with ill intent. "There it is", she announced and grinned her seductive smile at the Rosie Girls and Wander Groupies in attendance. Slink could slither her way into just about any close space and expand and contract certain body parts at will, that was her ability. Slink slid into the wedding dress and expanded her upper torso, ripping the inner seams. "Let me try", suggested a more endowed Rosie Girl who slipped on the stretched garment, stuck out her chest and tore the stitching to its limit. "That ought to cause an embarrassing wardrobe malfunction", announced Miss Slink. "I'd be soooo ashamed". The Rosie Girls and Wander Groupies giggled in wicked simultaneosity.

Arriving on the scene was Glimpz and company. Rump first, legs in the air, Glimpz's landing toppled Slink and the Rosie Girl. "Cannonball", yelled dog. A maylay ensued. "You leave Sue out of this!", exclaimed Horker, no one knowing exactly what he was talking about. "Take off that dress before any more garments get hurt", commanded Glimpz. "And what if I don't?", quizzed the Rosie Girl, and she was immediately tickled out of it by Glimpz and Turnip Oshanahee. "True to the way", commented Hogish Dog. "Triple T double U", agreed Glimpz as she tumbled sideways over and over with Slink. Turnip had the Rosie Girl by the ankle, dragging her in circles. "Let me in on some of that", stated Horker as he belly-flopped her torsoe, bouncing slightly. Referrer made for the Wander Groupies and remaining Rosie Girls, bowling ball to keg pin style. "You better not be liking that", cried Glimpz as she kneed Slink in the bottom, sliding off in the process. "I could use some help here". The Rosie girls and wander groupies aligned to Glimpz and company rushed to her aid. A violent struggle followed. There were human types and mutants disheveled everywhere. In a pile of bodies something disappeared and when the grouping disapated a loan travel pass was left on the floor. "I tried to tag her with it several times but it kept on slipping off. Good thing the crowd pressed in around her and kept it wedged to her", explained Glimpz. With Slink sent away the hoard unbanded rethinking their allegiances.

Sleekfur stayed on watch at the tux store with his crew awaiting any developments. Hairball paraded in with his group, containers of barber trimmings and animal shed in tow. "What will they do with that?", questioned one of Sleekfur's Angle Rangers. "I dread to think", answered Sleekfur and prepared for action. Hairball was quick, he had the containers open and clothes arranged in a matter of seconds. The tuxedos would not have a chance. Sleekfur was faster. He positioned himself next to the mischievous mutant just as the last plastic covering was removed. Hairball straightened to find himself face to face with Sleekfur. "Hellloo, Hairball", toned Sleekfur

"What cha' doin'?" The wiry outgrowth on hairball pointed in surprise. Hairball threw a faceful of mottled hair onto Sleekfur's bright, shiny coat causing him to howl in disgusted outrage. Avoiding the impending danger Sleekfur's forces gathered the chaste clothing and whisked them away out of danger. Sleekfur pinned Hairball's arms behind his back who jumped through and flipped Sleekfur. Sleekfur sideswiped Hairball's legs and applied a Yelpson maneuver. Hairball rolled through it. Hairball went for a paw to face. Sleekfur deflected it. The supporters of both sides found seats to watch the action. They all wanted to see this. Hairball turned sideways and slammed Sleekfur to the floor. Sleekfur looked done for. Hairball jumped in the air, arms and feet outstretched preparing to land horizontally on Sleekfur. Sleekfur rolled away. Hairball went splat, nose even with his cheekbones. Advantage Sleekfur. The crowd went ooo. Sleekfur put one leg between Hairball's, twisted him over like a pretzel and pulled back on Hairball's feet and neck. It was over. Hairball begged for the travel pass. Sleekfur obliged. The crowd shuffled away and Sleekfur pondered his returning pass amongst the congratulations of a few remaining teammates. "And so we live to protect for another day", commented Sleekfur. A rousing chorus of "true to the way" was heard. They trashed the ill-fated insulation and returned the esteemed garments to their originally fixed positions.

The Commemorative Glassware Factory was silent, eerily silent. Something was afoot as the sound of crunching crushed glass jarred the audible canals alerting LoudNote and crew to the disturbance. LoudNote quietly arranged his Rangers and Blokes to positions. This would be a tricky one. How do you stop a sound mutant from breaking glass when your own ability manipulates sound? StaticNoise could be heard across the room implementing his plan. He inhaled and prepared to let loose his sonic wave. Pow, piece of tape to the mouth as LoudNote taped his orifice, the pressure releasing harmlessly through his nostrils. Almost immediately the sound fiend tore off the obstruction and inhaled. Bam, taped shut again. Time after time the battle raged on until LoudNote reached the end of his role. Spying two warring rangers near the entrance LoudNote exclaimed, "Throw him through the door!", "It's the only way". LoudNote deflected the sound wave from StaticNoise out the open door and harmlessly to the surrounding area. Saving just enough energy to reach for his travel pass and pin StaticNoise, LoudNote wiggle-waved "bye" as the instrument of transport performed its duty. Returning with a clink, LoudNote returned the pass to its enclosure and escorted everyone out of the building. The factory was saved.

CHAPTER 8 - CEREMONY AND DIFFUSION

The time for betrothal was at hand. Everyone barfed. They were nervous. Baer strapped on his factory fresh tuxedo and proceeded to the vestibule of the Iron Cathedral. It was his turn to wait.

Romica, Handy Maidens in tow, proceeded curvaceously from the bride's room and awaited her entrance.

The ceremony started. Baer marched up the isle to the stone altar, dignified and formidable. The music continued, phase shifting for the bridal march.

Romica was a sight. The alteration department did a fine job. Bridal dress by Breckenridge in perfect uplifting condition.

"True to the way" exclaimed Bong from the congregation. Romica smiled.

Outside, in the parking lot, (yes, they had transportation) G.C. Gatorchomp was preparing his assault. "Where are they?", he grumbled to his two side guards. "They should have been here by now". Cee snickered from across the lot, knowing his assemblance of personnel would far outnumber any opposing threat from the other side. "Let's get this over with so we could enjoy the ceremony", said Cee to his gathering. As they began to appear from what seemed everywhere Geecy kicked at the ground and muttered something unrepeatable. "Bring the ramblecar", said Cee. "They'll run and we can't have them interfering with the ceremony or reception." "You really should learn more compassion for your fellow beings", commented Cee to Geecy who was barely in earshot. "I'm working on it", quipped Geecy, annoyed at the whole situation, his own ramblecar easing up to his side.

"We'll take the first watch", said Kitty Wampass, offering the services of husband and Anvils. Cee agreed, having them switch off with the mutant force so each could enjoy some of the festivities. Cee placed a small group at the lot, watched as the pursuit diminished in the distance and then went in to see the remainder of the ceremony. He liked throwing spice flowers on that happy couple as was customary on the steps at the end of the ceremony on their way to the reception. Great fun was to be had, the major threat diffused, a background of caution yet in place.

CHAPTER 9 - CELEBRATION

Romica bounced out of the rental ramble and with Baer hand-in-hand headed for the celebration. Everyone cheered as they entered Ornamental Hall. Romica went straight to the dance floor and shimmied and swayed herself into recognition. Baer drank beare, a local favorite and produced gutteral sounds as he watched his wife prance. The crowd filtered in, Cee and A Band sitting in sporadically with the resident locals. Roast sear sandwiches and a beare waterfall provided food and drink. A sparkling fall with chooseable flavorings for the younger and those less inclined. The families' elders produced toast after toast honoring the newly joined, a chorus of table thumpers chiming in to get the couple to kiss. A long celebrated garter ritual was performed. Turnip fainted at the sight. Many formed a circle and danced the Quacky Ack, a good way for people to get to know each other. The cake was three tiers and enjoyed by all. Nearing the end of the night Baer and Romica departed for their sweet evening. Cee sat back with his friends and pondered the latest events.

CHAPTER 10 - CONTEMPLATION

"Our ten rules plus those of men and mutant seem to be doing pretty well, a few adjustments here and there." Cee winked. "What defines a woman?" Beauty, lactal and orgasmic flow with womb? Feminine attitude? We'll leave the rib part out of it. It's also realized that some women have these things taken through no fault of their own."

"Let's figure out something for this over-population thing besides a war", Cee continued while still in a contemplative mood. "You people like to write rules and such. How about something that each person gets to replace themselves then it costs to have more. Maybe base it according to land mass and open land. 1/2 assigned to each parent of a child, a 1 total to replace themself."

Cee began a campaign to move 144 thousand at a time to more open areas of the three formations. Thus began the new age of the Tri-System.

Printed in the United States
by Baker & Taylor Publisher Services